# To Dad

First published in Great Britain in 2016 by Hodder and Stoughton

Text and illustrations copyright © Steve Antony, 2016

A CIP catalogue record of this book
is available from the British Library.

ISBN: 978 1 444 91667 6
10 9 8 7 6 5 4 3 2 1

Printed and bound in China

Hodder Children's Books
An imprint of
Hachette Children's Group
Part of Hodder and Stoughton
Carmelite House
50 Victoria Embankment
London EC4Y 0DZ

An Hachette UK Company
www.hachette.co.uk
www.hachettechildrens.co.uk

Hodder
Children's
Books

# I'll Wait, Mr Panda

Steve Antony

What are you making, Mr Panda?

Wait and see. It's a surprise.

No, I will not wait.
Goodbye.

I'll wait,
Mr Panda.

Are you
making cookies,
Mr Panda?

Wait and see. It's a surprise.

No, waiting
is too hard.
Goodbye.

I'll wait, Mr Panda.

No,
I'm done
waiting.

Is it ready yet, Mr Panda?

No, wait here.

I don't like waiting.

Goodbye.

# I'll Wait,
## Mr Panda!

I'm waiting, Mr Panda.

WOW!
That was worth the wait.

I know.

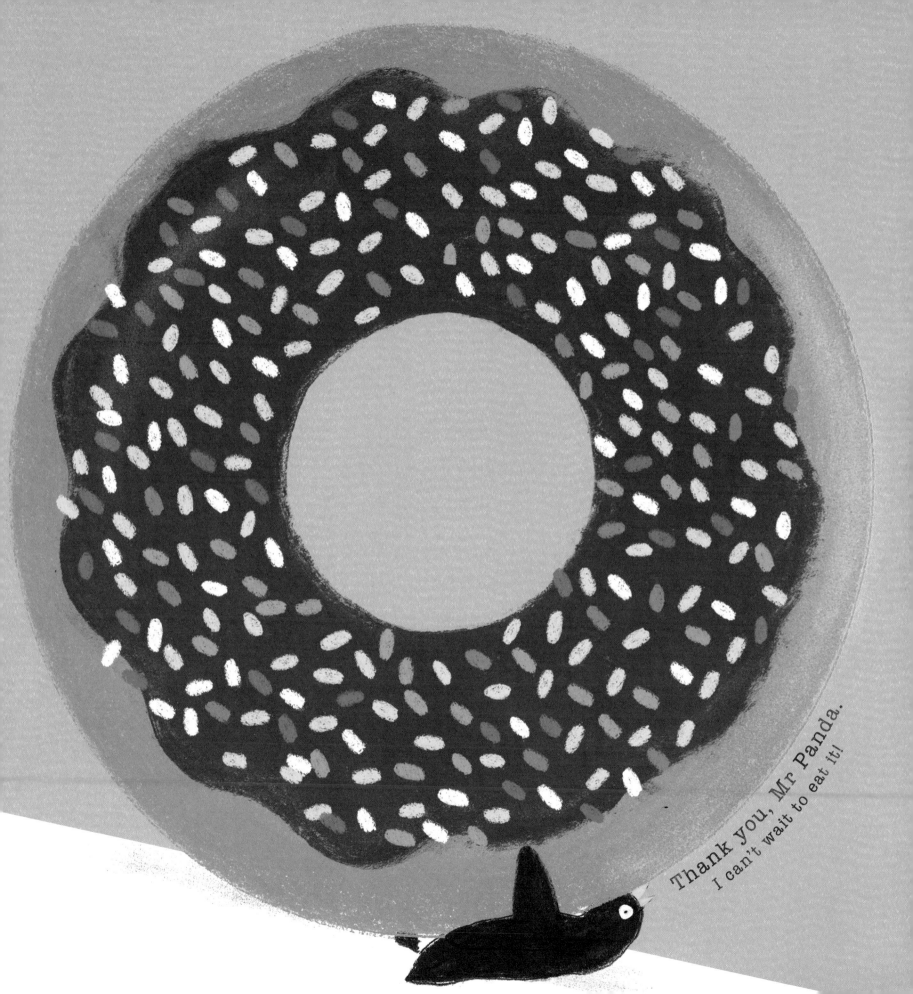

Thank you, Mr Panda.
I can't wait to eat it!

# More fantastic books from
## Steve Antony...